Willy the Dinosaur Lies

by Wayne Triebwasser, Ed.D. & Elizabeth Squires, Ed.S.
illustrations by Lisbeth J. Solum

Publisher—

Educational Media Corporation®
P.O. Box 21311
Minneapolis, MN 55421-0311

(763) 781-0088 or (800) 966-3382

www.**educationalmedia**.com

Production editor—
Don L. Sorenson

Graphic design—
Earl Sorenson

Illustrations—
Lisbeth J. Solum

Willy discovers lying is no way to make friends. How does Willy turn his life around? Read this book and find out.

"I can get out of anything by lying," Willy says to himself.

"Willy! Did you clean your room?" asks his mother. "Yes, Mom!" says Willy.

Willy's mom goes to check on his room. "What a mess!" she exclaims.

"Willy, did you do your homework?" asks his mother. "I sure did!" says Willy.

"Where is your homework, Willy?" asks his teacher.
"On the way to school, a dog grabbed it and ran away," he answers.

"It's easy to make friends by lying," Willy boasts to himself.

"My dad makes so much money he puts it in different banks. One bank isn't big enough to hold it all," he says to some kids in the lunch room.

A classmate asks Willy, "Why don't you go out for wrestling?"

"I want to give other kids a chance. At my last school, I was never beaten," replies Willy.

Willy continues to lie. "I catch fish so big there isn't a big enough scale to weigh them," he brags.

A neighbor has a birthday party. Someone asks, "Where is Willy?"

"I didn't invite him," says the birthday boy. "Who can stand Willy? He never tells the truth!"

The neighbor ladies meet for a coffee party. They like to talk about their kids. "My daughter is *so* popular," brags one lady.

"My son is *so* good at sports," says another.

"Willy is such a good boy. He always tells the truth,"
Willy's mother states proudly.

At home, Willy is very lonely. He can't understand why he is not invited to anyone's house.

Some kids tell him what he doesn't want to hear. "You will never have any friends, because you don't tell the truth!"

Burt, Willy's neighbor, sees Willy sitting alone on his front step. "What is the problem, Willy?" asks Burt.

"Everything is just fine," answers Willy, as tears roll down his face.

The next day, Burt decides to talk with Willy. "You are always alone," says Burt.

"I have lots of friends," replies Willy.

"Willy, please tell the truth," urges Burt.

"No one likes me," cries Willy. "I am all alone."

"Now you are telling the truth," replies Burt.

Burt continues, "Tell the truth, Willy. People will trust you if you tell the truth. Start by admitting you are not perfect. No one is perfect."

"Is it really that easy?" asks Willy.

"Sure," says Burt.

The next day at lunch, Willy talks to Matt. He admits he does not know everything. Matt notices a change in Willy and invites him to his house.

After school, Matt shows Willy his fishing rods and reels. Willy listens to Matt and does not stretch the truth by bragging and boasting about himself.

A few days later, Burt continues to encourage Willy. "It's going better? Great! Now, try something new." urges Burt. "Tell the truth about *your feelings*. Willy, share how you feel with others."

Willy decides to tell his new friend, Tyler, the truth about how he *feels*. "I can't stand being alone."

"You don't have to be alone," Tyler replies. "We are having a party at my house this weekend. You are invited to come, Willy."

Willy's classmates begin talking about him. "Willy is a great guy," says one classmate.

"I like him when he tells the truth," says another.

Willy attends the party at Tyler's house. Everyone has a great time, including Willy.

Willy decides to try telling the truth to his teacher. "I haven't been doing my homework," he says.

"Well, why not start today, Willy, with a promise to yourself to do your homework?" she says.

There is one more place to try out this truth stuff—at home. Willy's mom says, "Willy, did you clean your room?"

"Nope," answers Willy, "But I will."

"That's fine," Willy's mom replies. "Thanks for telling the truth."

"How is it going?" asks Burt.

"Great," says Willy.

Burt continues, "Remember, Willy, try to tell the truth. People will trust you if you tell the truth. You can start by admitting you are not perfect. No one is perfect. Tell the truth about your feelings. Remember, if you want to have friends, tell the truth."

"Willy, you are doing great! I knew you could do it!"
says Burt as he drives away.

"Life is great when you tell the truth," Willy says to his friend.